Thanks to the Animals

Allen Sockabasin

Passamaquoddy Storyteller

Illustrated by Rebekah Raye

Winter had arrived.
Joo Tum worked for days preparing
for the trip north with his family.

He took apart their house near the shore
and stacked the cedar logs on the big bobsled.

Everyone helped.

They packed the family sled
    with his tools and with the meats and fish and vegetables
        harvested during the summer, when the days were long.

It was loaded to the very top with precious food,
    but Joo Tum made sure there was room
        for his children to ride in the back.

Everyone dressed in warm sealskin clothes
for the long trip.
It was time to go to their winter home
in the deep woods.
The horses pulled the sled slowly through the new snow.

Zoo Sap was not yet walking,
        but he was a strong baby, born in the spring.
He rode on the sled with the other children.

As the shadows grew long, the older children slept.
But then little Zoo Sap stood up and tumbled off the sled!

Oh, how Zoo Sap cried! His voice filled the sky.

The animals of the forest were alerted by his crying.
First to come were the beaver.
They knew they had to keep him warm and dry,
so they put their tails together and cradled Zoo Sap.

Zoo Sap still cried, so the moose came.
Then the bear, the caribou, and the deer.
The fox and the wolf came, too.
And all the big animals lay together in a circle.

Then the other, smaller animals came—
the raccoons, porcupines, rabbits, weasels, and mink.
The muskrat and otter and the squirrels and mice came, too.

They gathered and filled in the cracks
                 between the big animals.

At sunset the owl came.

Then the raven, crow, jay, duck, and a goose
gathered to perch on top.

Even a seagull came.

Last came the great bald eagle,
who spread her wings over all the other birds and animals.
Zoo Sap stayed warm.

When Joo Tum arrived at his winter home
he knew something was very wrong.

Zoo Sap was missing.

Joo Tum quickly lit a fire for his family
and got them settled.
Then he turned back to the trail to find his son.

He traveled through the woods all night,
and just at sunrise he came to a big mound of snow.
Resting on top was the great bald eagle.

"I knew you would come back for Zoo Sap," the eagle said.
Joo Tum looked down and saw his son,
safely sleeping in a great pile of warm animals.

Joo Tum thanked the animals one by one.
Then he took Zoo Sap in his strong arms
and went back to the family.

When they arrived that evening,
there was feasting and dancing.

What a celebration!

THE PASSAMAQUODDY LANGUAGE IS STILL SPOKEN BY MANY members of the tribe, and there are ongoing efforts to increase the number of tribal children who speak their native language. Once, the Passamaquoddy and related tribes occupied land between Maine and New Brunswick, Canada. Today there are approximately 3,200 tribal members and the tribe owns 142,000 acres of land in Maine, which it monitors and maintains. Many Passamaquoddy live at Zee-byig (Pleasant Point) on Passamaquoddy Bay, or at Mud-doc-mig-goog (Indian Township) near the St. Croix River.

If you would like to hear Allen Sockabasin reading this story in Passamaquoddy, please go to our website at www.tilburyhouse.com.

Below are the Passamaquoddy names for the animals in this book, spelled phonetically by Allen to help English-speaking people become familiar with Passamaquoddy as it has been spoken traditionally.

Beaver	Qua-bid
Moose	Mooz
Bear	Moo-ween
Caribou	Mug-ga-lib
Deer	Aduke
Fox	Quawk-sus
Wolf	Mull-sun
Raccoon	Ess-puhns
Porcupine	Mudd-wehs
Rabbit	Ma-art-teh-gwas
Weasel	Zerg-whehs
Mink	G-yauh-kehs
Otter	Kiw-nigg
Muskrat	Kiw-huzz
Squirrel	Meek-koo
Mouse	Obb-biwqk-saz
Owl	Koo-kook-huz
Raven	Kchee-gah-gog
Crow	Gah-gah-koos
Canadian jay	Pskun-quahs
Duck	Mud-heh-sim
Goose	Wub-tuwqk-heig
Eagle	Jeep-law-gun

TILBURY HOUSE, PUBLISHERS
103 Brunswick Ave.
Gardiner, Maine 04345
800–582–1899
www.tilburyhouse.com

First hardcover printing: July 2005 • 10 9 8 7 6 5 4
First paperback printing:

Dedications
This book is dedicated to my mom, Molly Zoo-Sap,
for many of my stories. —AJS
To Kenny for his love and thoughtful understanding,
and for my family. —RR

Library of Congress Cataloging-in-Publication Data

Sockabasin, Allen, 1944-
   Thanks to the animals / by Allen Sockabasin ; illustrated by Rebekah Raye.
      p. cm.
   Summary: In 1900 during the Passamaquoddy winter migration in Maine, Baby Zoo Sap falls off the family bobsled and the forest animals hearing his cries, gather to protect him until his father returns to find him.
   ISBN 978-0-88448-270-3 (hardcover : alk. paper)
   [1. Babies--Fiction. 2. Forest animals—Fiction. 3. Passamaquoddy Indians—Fiction. 4. Indians of North America—Maine—Fiction. 5. Maine—History—20th century—Fiction.]
I. Raye, Rebekah, ill. II. Title.
   PZ7.S685252Th 2005
   [E]--dc22
                                    2004029039

Designed by Geraldine Millham, Westport, Massachusetts.
Editing and production by Audrey Maynard, Jennifer Bunting, and Barbara Diamond.
Printed by Sung In Printing, Gyeonggi, South Korea, August 2009